I dedicate my part of this book

————— *to* —————

Rosemary Wells

in return for the great pleasure

she has given me

with her part of the book

IONA OPIE

————— *For* —————

Rosemary Sandberg

ROSEMARY WELLS

MY VERY FIRST
MOTHER GOOSE

edited by
IONA OPIE

illustrated by
ROSEMARY WELLS

CANDLEWICK PRESS
CAMBRIDGE, MASSACHUSETTS

MOTHER GOOSE,

that kind and quizzical old lady, knows all about human nature. For centuries she has been gathering rhymes that will help people along the bumpy road of life. "If they fall down," she says, "it is only to be expected—Jack and Jill fell down, too." I imagine her sitting beside a large sack full of glistening versicles: "A two-year-old in a temper? 'Davy Davy Dumpling' would be just the thing. A grizzling three-year-old on a rainy afternoon? I recommend a dance or two—'Sally go round the sun,' perhaps, with 'Shoo fly' to follow." What treasures she has! Places to go to, and places to come back to: "Over the hills and far away," then home to tea by the fireside with a welcome "Three good wishes" and "Three good kisses." Remedies for people who do not want to go to bed: "Up the wooden hill to Blanket Fair"; and for people who do not want to get up: "Elsie Marley's grown so fine." Jollifications that cheer parents as well as children: like "Dance to your daddy" and "Hi! Hi! says Anthony."

There they lie, the nursery rhymes, so much at the back of our minds that we can't remember when we first learned them. What did they give us, so long ago? A suggestion that mishaps might be funny rather than tragic, that tantrums can be comical as well as frightening, and that laughter is the cure for practically everything.

We seem to be born, too, with a love for music and the music of words (try singing "Boys and girls come out to play" to a baby of three months old). But introductions must be made. The words one first meets in nursery rhymes will always have a special magic, all the stronger for being mysterious and incomprehensible; and what pleasanter way to learn your numbers than through the black sheep's allocation of his bags of wool, or the enumeration of Mrs. Hen's diversely colored chickens.

I firmly believe that Rosemary Wells is Mother Goose's second cousin and has inherited the family point of view. Her illustrations exactly reflect Mother Goose's many moods: glumpish, her animals look wickedly askance at the world; happy, they almost dance off the page; cosily at home, there is no greater depth of content-ment. They make me shout with glee. She has learned the family secrets, too. Even I had never heard the full story of "Cobbler, cobbler, mend my shoe," or knew that when the mouse ran down the clock, the cat was close by, asleep in his armchair.

Mother Goose will show newcomers to this world how astonishing, beautiful, capricious, dancy, eccentric, funny, goluptious, haphazard, intertwingled, joyous, kindly, loving, melodious, naughty, outrageous, pomsidillious, querimonious, romantic, silly, tremendous, unexpected, vertiginous, wonderful, x-citing, yo-heave-ho-ish, and zany it is. And when we come to be grandmothers, it is just as well to be reminded of these twenty-six attributes.

Iona Opie

Jerry Hall,

He is so small,

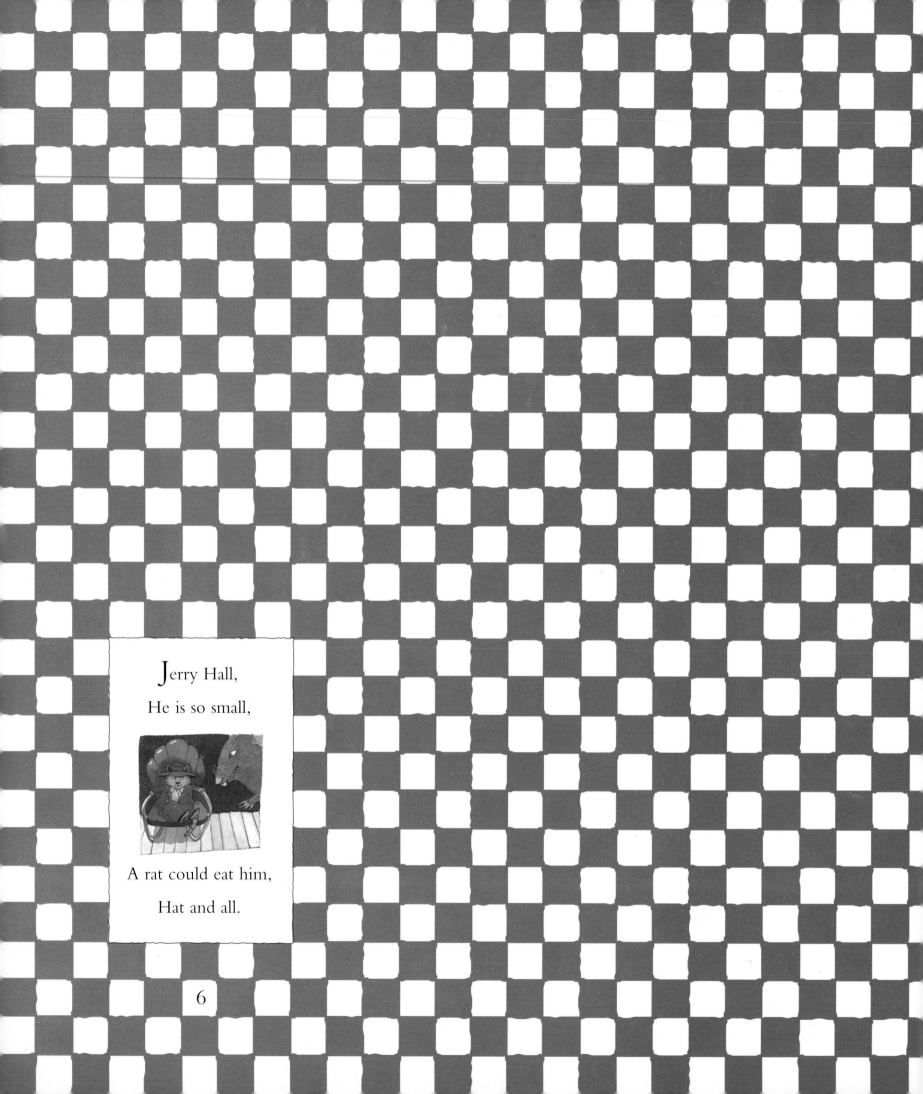

A rat could eat him,

Hat and all.

Contents

Tom he was a piper's son,

He learned to play

   when he was young,

But all the tunes

   that he could play

Was Over the hills

   and far away,

Over the hills

   and a great way off,

The wind shall blow

   my topknot off.

Chapter One
Jack and Jill

Jack and Jill went up the hill,
To fetch a pail of water;

Jack fell down and broke his crown,
And Jill came tumbling after.

Shoo fly, don't bother me,
Shoo fly, don't bother me,

Shoo fly, don't bother me,
I belong to somebody.

Boys and girls
 come out to play,
The moon doth shine
 as bright as day.
Leave your supper
 and leave your sleep,
And join your playfellows
 in the street.

Come with a whoop,
 and come with a call,
Come with a good will
 or not at all.
Up the ladder
 and down the wall,
A tuppenny loaf
 will serve us all.
You bring milk
 and I'll bring flour,
And we'll have a pudding
 in half an hour.

Humpty Dumpty sat on a wall,

Humpty Dumpty had a great fall.

All the king's horses and all the king's men

Couldn't put Humpty together again.

Down at the station, early in the morning,

See the little puffer-billies all in a row;

See the engine driver pull his little lever—

Puff puff, peep peep, off we go!

Baa, baa, black sheep,

have you any wool?

Yes, sir, yes, sir,

three bags full.

One for the master,
  and one for the dame,
And one for the little boy
  who lives down the lane.

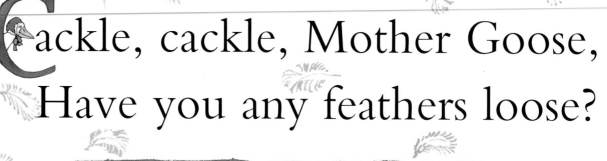

Cackle, cackle, Mother Goose,
Have you any feathers loose?

20

Truly have I, pretty fellow,
Quite enough to fill a pillow.

To market, to market, to buy a fat pig,
Home again, home again, jiggety-jig.

To market, to market, to buy a fat hog,
Home again, home again, jiggety-jog.

Wash the dishes,
Wipe the dishes,
Ring the bell for tea;

Three good wishes,
Three good kisses,
I will give to thee.

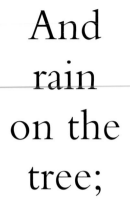ain
on the
green
grass,

And
rain
on the
tree;

Rain
on the
house
top,

But not on me.

Warm hands, warm,
The men are gone to plow,
If you want to warm your hands,
Warm your hands now.

Ride a cockhorse to Banbury Cross
To see a fine lady on a white horse;
Rings on her fingers and bells on her toes,
She shall have music wherever she goes.

Trot, trot, to Boston; trot, trot, to Lynn;
Trot, trot, to Salem; home, home, again.

Horsie, horsie, don't you stop,
Just let your feet go clipetty clop;
Your tail goes swish, and the wheels go round—
Giddyup, you're homeward bound!

Father and Mother
and Uncle John,
Went to market one by one;
Father fell off—!
And Mother fell off—!

But Uncle John—
Went on, and on,
and on, and on . . .

and on, and on, and on . . .

Chapter Two
Hey Diddle, Diddle

Hey diddle, diddle,

the cat and the fiddle,

The cow jumped over the moon;

The little dog laughed

to see such fun,

And the dish ran away

with the spoon.

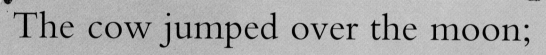

Sing a song of sixpence,
A pocket full of rye;
Four and twenty blackbirds
Baked in a pie.
When the pie was opened,
The birds began to sing;
Wasn't that a dainty dish
To set before the king?

Smiling girls, rosy boys,
Come and buy my little toys:
Monkeys made
of gingerbread
And sugar horses
painted red.

Handy spandy,
sugary candy,
French almond rock;
Bread and butter
for your supper,
That is all your
mother's got.

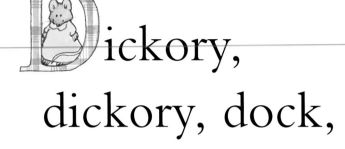ickory,
dickory, dock,

The mouse ran
up the clock.

The clock struck one,
The mouse ran down,

Dickory,
dickory, dock.

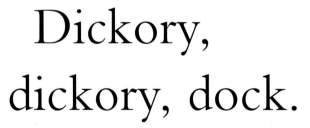

ickory,
dickory, dare,
The pig flew up
in the air.

The man in brown
Soon brought him down,

Dickory,
dickory, dare.

There was a crooked man,

And he walked a crooked mile,

He found a crooked sixpence

Against a crooked stile.

He bought a crooked cat,

Which caught a crooked mouse,

And they all lived together

In a little crooked house.

The cock's on the housetop, blowing his horn;

The bull's in the barn, a-threshing the corn;

The maids in the meadow are making the hay;

The ducks in the river are swimming away.

Pat-a-cake, pat-a-cake, baker's man,
Bake me a cake as fast as you can;
Pat it and prick it, and mark it with T,
Put it in the oven for Tommy and me.

Davy Davy Dumpling,

Boil him in a pot;

Sugar him and butter him,

And eat him while he's hot.

Little Jack Horner sat in a corner,

Eating his Christmas pie;

He put in his thumb, and pulled out a plum,

And said, What a good boy am I!

48

Hi! Hi! says Anthony,

Puss is in the pantry,

Gnawing, gnawing,

A mutton mutton-bone;

See how she tumbles it,

See how she mumbles it,

See how she tosses

The mutton mutton-bone.

Sing, sing,

What shall I sing?

The cat's run away

With the pudding string!

Do, do,

What shall I do?

The cat's run away

With the pudding too!

Hickety, pickety, my black hen,

She lays eggs for gentlemen;

Gentlemen come every day

To see what my black hen doth lay.

Elsie Marley's grown so fine,

She won't get up to feed the swine,

But lies in bed till eight or nine.

Lazy Elsie Marley.

Pussycat, pussycat, where have you been?
I've been to London to look at the queen.

Pussycat, pussycat, what did you there?

I frightened a little mouse under her chair.

ance to your daddy,   You shall have a fishy

My little babby,   In a little dishy,

Dance to your daddy,   You shall have a fishy

My little lamb.   When the boat comes in.

Puss came dancing
out of a barn
With a pair of bagpipes
under her arm;

She could sing nothing
but Fiddle cum fee,
The mouse has married
the bumblebee . . .

Pipe, cat!

Dance, mouse!

We'll have a wedding

at our good house.

Chapter Three
Little Jumping Joan

Here am I, Little Jumping Joan;
When nobody's with me, I'm all alone.

I had a little nut tree, nothing would it bear
But a silver nutmeg and a golden pear.

The king of Spain's daughter came to visit me,
And all for the sake of my little nut tree.

I skipped over water, I danced over sea,
And all the birds in the air couldn't catch me.

Up the wooden hill to Blanket Fair,

What shall we have when we get there?

A bucket full of water

And a pennyworth of hay,

Gee up, Dobbin,

All the way!

If I had a donkey
that wouldn't go,

D'you think I'd beat him?
Oh, no, no.

I'd put him in a barn
and give him some corn,

The best little donkey
that ever was born.

From **Wibbleton** to **Wobbleton** is fifteen miles,

From **Wobbleton** to **Wibbleton** is fifteen miles,

64

From **Wibbleton** to **Wobbleton**, from **Wobbleton** to **Wibbleton**,

From **Wibbleton** to **Wobbleton** is fifteen miles.

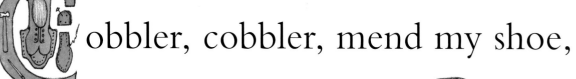

Cobbler, cobbler, mend my shoe,

Get it done by half-past two;

Half-past two is much too late,

Get it done by half-past eight.

Stitch it up and stitch it down,

Then I'll give you half a crown.

One, two, three, four,

Mary's at the cottage door,

Five, six, seven, eight,

Eating cherries off a plate.

One
for
sorrow

Two
for
joy

Three
for a
girl

Four
for a
boy

Five
for
silver

Six
for
gold

Seven
for a
secret

Ne'er
to be
told.

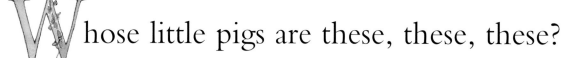

Whose little pigs are these, these, these?
Whose little pigs
are these?

They are Roger the Cook's,
I know by their looks—

I found them among my peas.

Oh, the brave old duke of York,
He had ten thousand men;
He marched them up to the top of the hill,
And he marched them down again.
And when they were up, they were up,
And when they were down, they were down,
And when they were only halfway up,
They were neither up nor down.

rs. Mason
bought a basin;

Mrs. Tyson said,

What a nice 'un;

What did it cost?

said Mrs. Frost;

Half a crown,

said Mrs. Brown;

Did it indeed?

said Mrs. Reed;

It did for certain,

said Mrs. Burton . . .

Then

Mrs. Nix

up to her

tricks

Threw the

basin on the

bricks.

Half a pound of tuppenny rice,
Half a pound of treacle,
Mix it up and make it nice—
POP goes the weasel!

Ms. Greta Grizzly
Beartown
USA
50194

A penny for a spool of thread,
A penny for a needle,
That's the way the money goes—
Pop goes the weasel!!

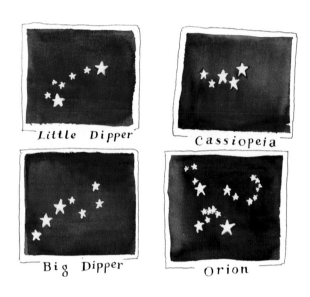

Little Dipper   Cassiopeia

Big Dipper   Orion

Star light, star bright,
First star I see tonight,
I wish I may, I wish I might,
Have the wish I wish tonight.

Sally go round the sun, Sally go round the moon, Sally go round the chimney pots on a Sunday afternoon.

Chapter Four

The Moon Sees Me

I see the moon,

And the moon sees me;

God bless the moon,

And God bless me.

The wind, the wind, the wind blows high,
The rain comes scattering down the sky.

She is handsome, she is pretty,
She is the girl of the golden city.

She goes a-courting, one, two, three,
Please and tell me who is she.

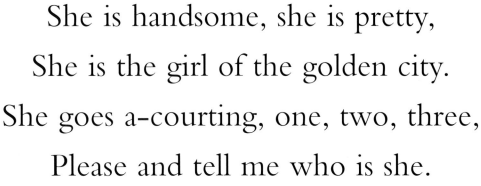

Blow, wind, blow!

And go, mill, go!

That the miller
may grind
his corn;
That the baker
may take it,
And into bread
make it,

And bring us a loaf
in the morn.

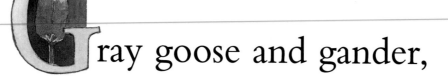ray goose and gander,

Waft your wings together,

And carry the good king's daughter

Over the one-strand river.

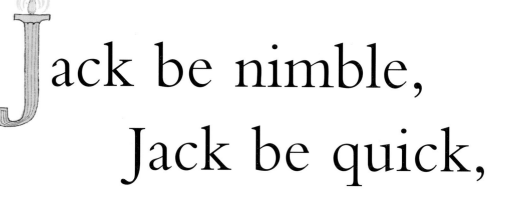 Jack be nimble,
Jack be quick,

Jack jump over
The candlestick.

The man in the moon

Came down too soon,

And asked his way

to Norwich;

He went by the south

And burnt his mouth

With supping cold

plum porridge.

Milkman, milkman,

where have you been?

In Buttermilk Channel up to my chin.

I spilled my milk, and I spoiled my clothes,

And I got a long icicle hung from my nose.

on again off again on again on again off again on again off again on again off again

Polly put the kettle on,

Polly put the kettle on,

Polly put the kettle on,

We'll all have tea.

94

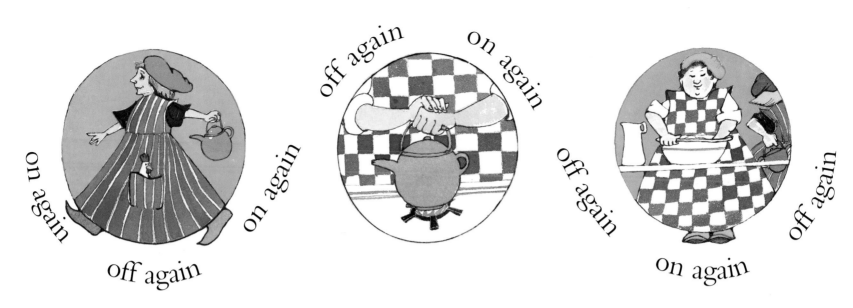

Sukey take it off again,

Sukey take it off again,

Sukey take it off again,

They've all gone away.

I'll buy you a tartan bonnet,
And feathers to put upon it,

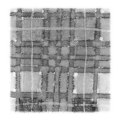

Buchanan

MacLeod

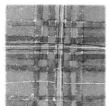

Stewart

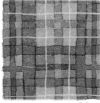

McNeill

With a hush-a-bye and a lullaby,
Because you are so like your daddy.

Wee Willie Winkie
runs
through
the town,
Upstairs and
downstairs
in his
nightgown,

Rapping at the window,
crying through the lock,
Are the children all in bed,
for now it's eight o'clock?

Matthew, Mark, Luke, and John,

Bless the bed that I lie on.

Four angels round my bed;

Two of them stand at my head,

Two of them stand at my feet,

All will watch me while I sleep.

The big ship

sails on

the alley

alley oh,

The alley

alley oh,

the alley

alley oh;

The big ship
sails on
the alley
alley oh,
On the last
day of
September.

How many miles to Babylon?
Threescore and ten.
Can I get there by candlelight?
Yes, and back again.

Open your gates as wide as the sky
And let the king and his men pass by.

Matthew, Mark, Luke, and John,

Hold my horse till I leap on;

Hold him steady, hold him sure,

And I'll get over the misty moor.

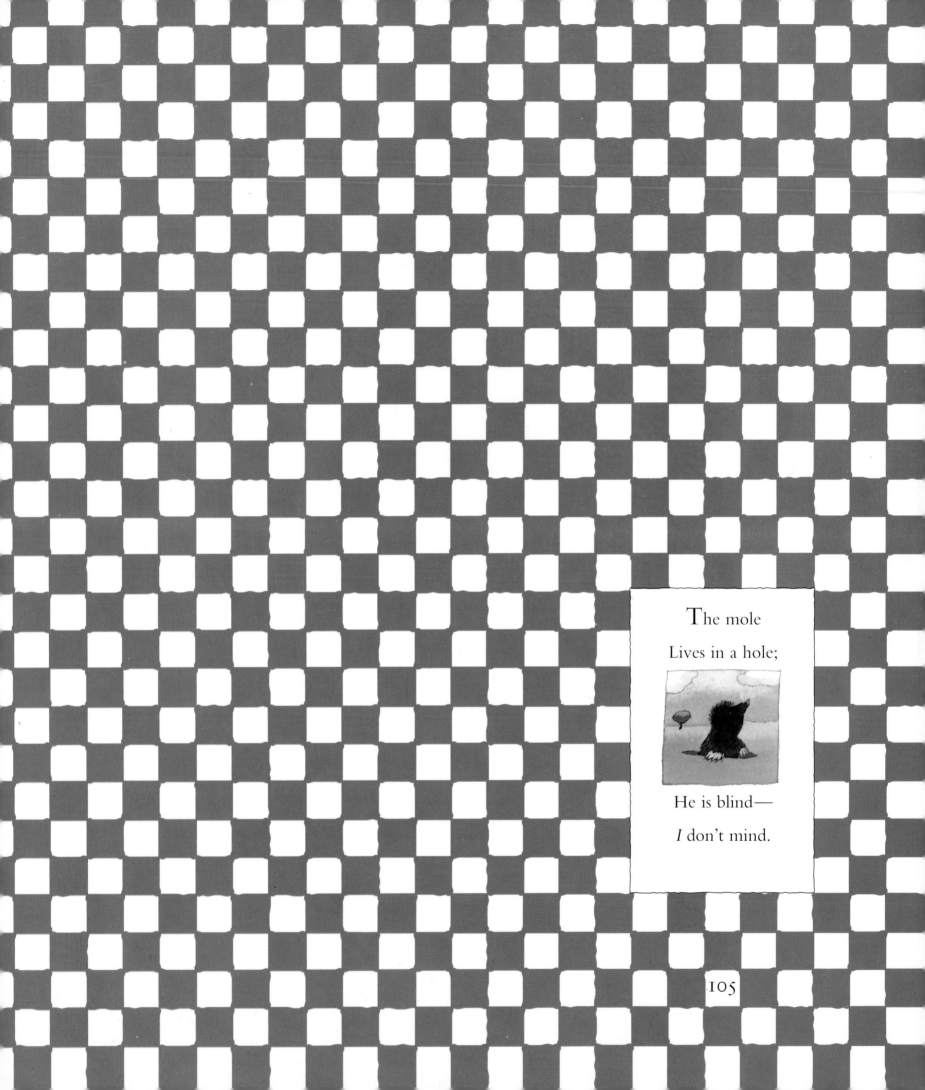

The mole

Lives in a hole;

He is blind—

I don't mind.

105

Index of First Lines

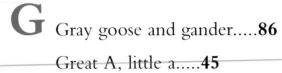

Compiled text copyright © 1996 by Iona Opie
Illustrations copyright © 1996 by Rosemary Wells

All rights reserved.

First U.S. edition 1996

Library of Congress Cataloging-in-Publication Data

My very first Mother Goose / edited by Iona Opie ;
illustrated by Rosemary Wells.—1st U.S. ed.
Summary: A collection of more than sixty nursery rhymes,
including "Hey Diddle, Diddle," "Pat-a-Cake,"
"Little Jack Horner," and "Pussycat, Pussycat."
ISBN 1-56402-620-5
1. Nursery rhymes. 2. Children's poetry. [1. Nursery rhymes.]
I. Opie, Iona Archibald. II. Wells, Rosemary, ill. III. Mother Goose.
PZ8.3.M9926   1996
398.8—dc20   96-4904

8 10 9 7

Printed in Italy

This book was typeset in M Bembo.
The pictures were done in watercolor and ink.

Candlewick Press
2067 Massachusetts Avenue
Cambridge, Massachusetts 02140

This edition published exclusively
for **Discovery Toys, Inc.**